The Many Adventures of Grandpa and Grandpa's Girl

SWIM

DRIVE

SLEEP

WE CAN...

FLY

VINCENT N. SCIALO

Illustrations by
Joseph C. Pepe and Jennifer Scialo

AuthorHouse™
1663 Liberty Drive
Bloomington, IN 47403
www.authorhouse.com
Phone: 1 (833) 262-8899

Because of the dynamic nature of the Internet, any web addresses or links contained in this book may have changed
since publication and may no longer be valid. The views expressed in this work are solely those of the author and do
not necessarily reflect the views of the publisher, and the publisher hereby disclaims any responsibility for them.

Any people depicted in stock imagery provided by Getty Images are models,
and such images are being used for illustrative purposes only.
Certain stock imagery © Getty Images.

This book is printed on acid-free paper.

ISBN: 978-1-6655-0468-3 (sc)
ISBN: 978-1-6655-0469-0 (e)

Print information available on the last page.

Published by AuthorHouse 10/28/2020

authorHOUSE®

THE MANY ADVENTURES of GRANDPA and GRANDPA'S GIRL

by

VINCENT N. SCIALO

ILLUSTRATIONS by:

Great-Grandpa, Joseph C. Pepe and
Grandma, Jennifer Scialo

For Emma:

You make me smile and laugh each and every day, and fill my heart with overflowing LOVE!

-Grandpa Vin

For Emma:

Just when I thought I could love no other.... along came my granddaughter Emma.

-Grandma Jen

For Emma:

GREAT GRAND FATHERS feel great because of Beautiful Great Grand Daughters like you.

-Great Grandpa Papa Joe

Other books by Vincent N. Scialo

The Rocking Chair
Randolph's Tale (A Journey for Love)
Deep In The Woods
Heigh-Ho
Not By Choice
Journey Every Step Un-Sure
The Decision

WE CAN SWIM

"Grandpa, Grandpa… Why can fish swim under the
sea and how come not you and me?"
"Close your eyes and hold your breath,
we're diving down to such a great depth."

Down...

Down...

Down...

"Down and deeper we go,
To the bottom of the ocean where it
can never snow!!"

2

"Oh, Grandpa... look around...
There's starfish, jellyfish and
so much more to be found!"

"Keep moving your feet to the beat of the
ocean, you got it Grandpa's girl,
can't you feel all the motion?"
"I can open my mouth and no water comes in...
I feel like a fish but I don't have any fins."

"Grandpa, Grandpa… What's that up ahead?"

"I believe it's an eel, that is starting to shed."

"Let's keep flapping our arms so we can continue

to move, you got it now, you're into the groove."

A whale of such enormous size swims past, swishing it's tail to make it move fast.

"Duck, Duck and watch your head, there's no stopping us now, but you should be in bed."

"We'll swim past these rocks and over these reefs, what's swimming this way shouldn't give us any grief."

A dozen or more dolphins galore, off in the distance there seems to be more.

"Grandpa, Grandpa… they're such a pretty gray. I want to be a dolphin hopefully one day. I'll watch over all the other fish, that will be my greatest wish. I want my legs to also go swish….."

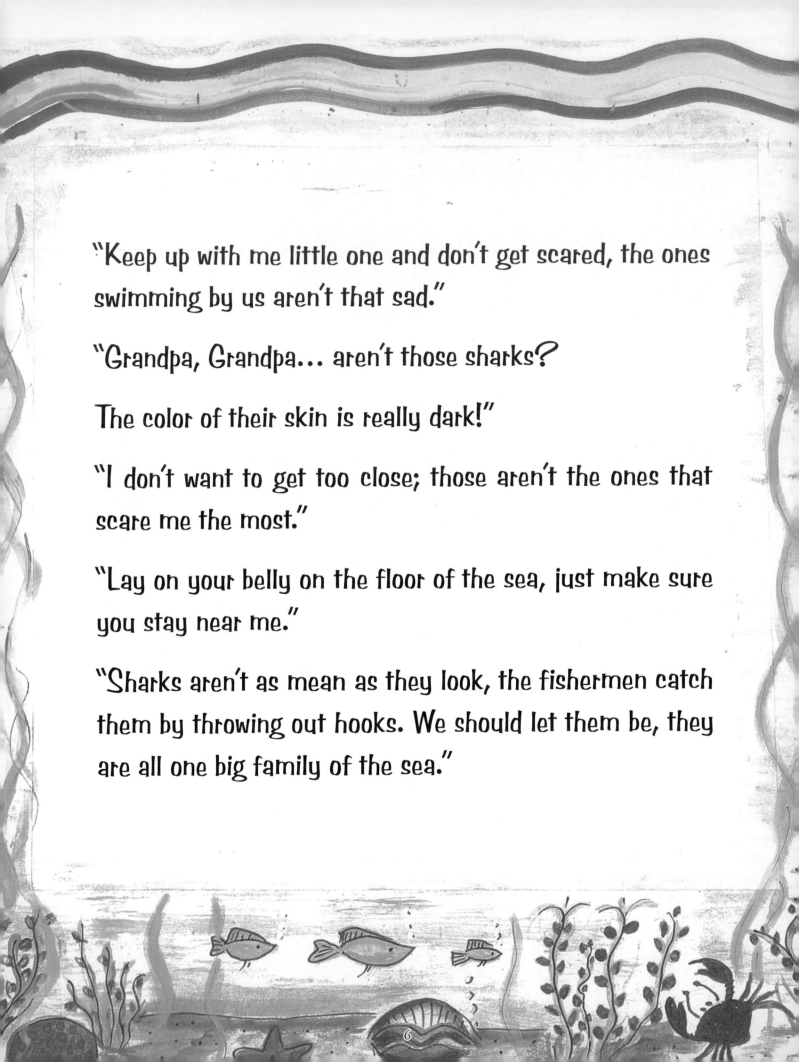

"Keep up with me little one and don't get scared, the ones swimming by us aren't that sad."

"Grandpa, Grandpa... aren't those sharks?

The color of their skin is really dark!"

"I don't want to get too close; those aren't the ones that scare me the most."

"Lay on your belly on the floor of the sea, just make sure you stay near me."

"Sharks aren't as mean as they look, the fishermen catch them by throwing out hooks. We should let them be, they are all one big family of the sea."

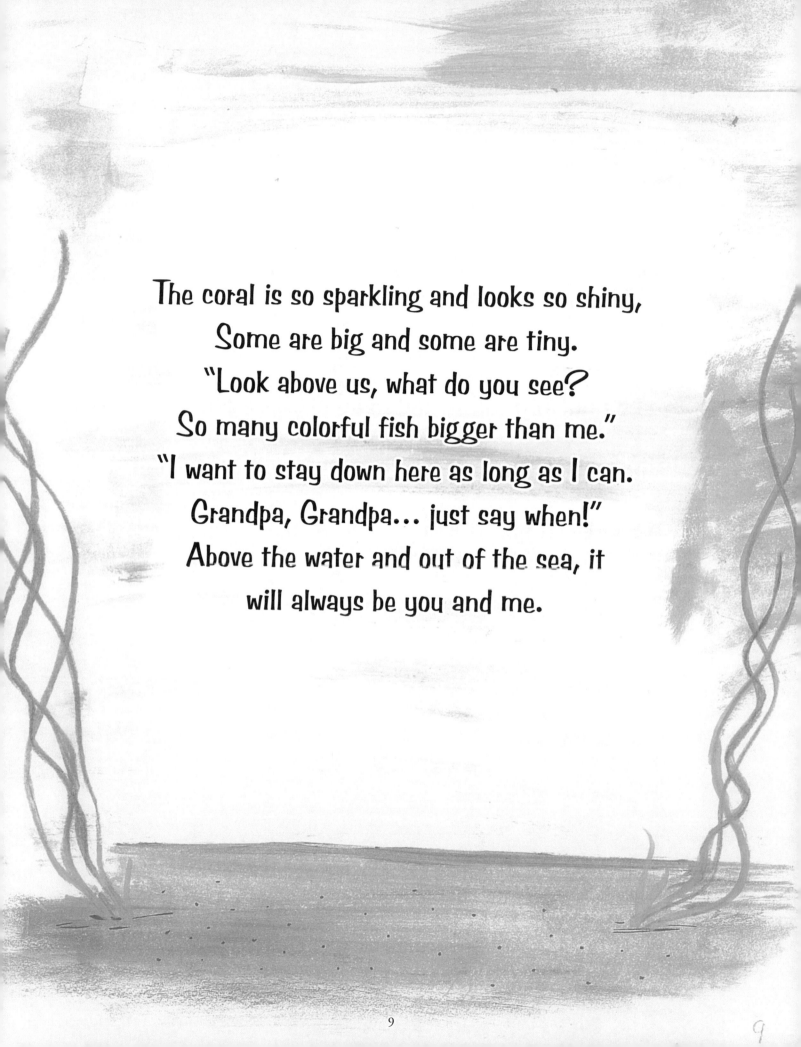

The coral is so sparkling and looks so shiny,
Some are big and some are tiny.
"Look above us, what do you see?
So many colorful fish bigger than me."
"I want to stay down here as long as I can.
Grandpa, Grandpa... just say when!"
Above the water and out of the sea, it
will always be you and me.

"Oh Grandpa, Grandpa… was this only a test?"

"No, no my little one, there will be so much more.
Let's float to the top and head back to your door."

With a splash from their feet and back on the land,

Grandpa finally let's go of her hand.

Placing her gently in her bed, Grandpa
reaches over and kisses her head.
And with a long sigh…
He states "you need to get some rest.
Grandpa will always love you the best!"

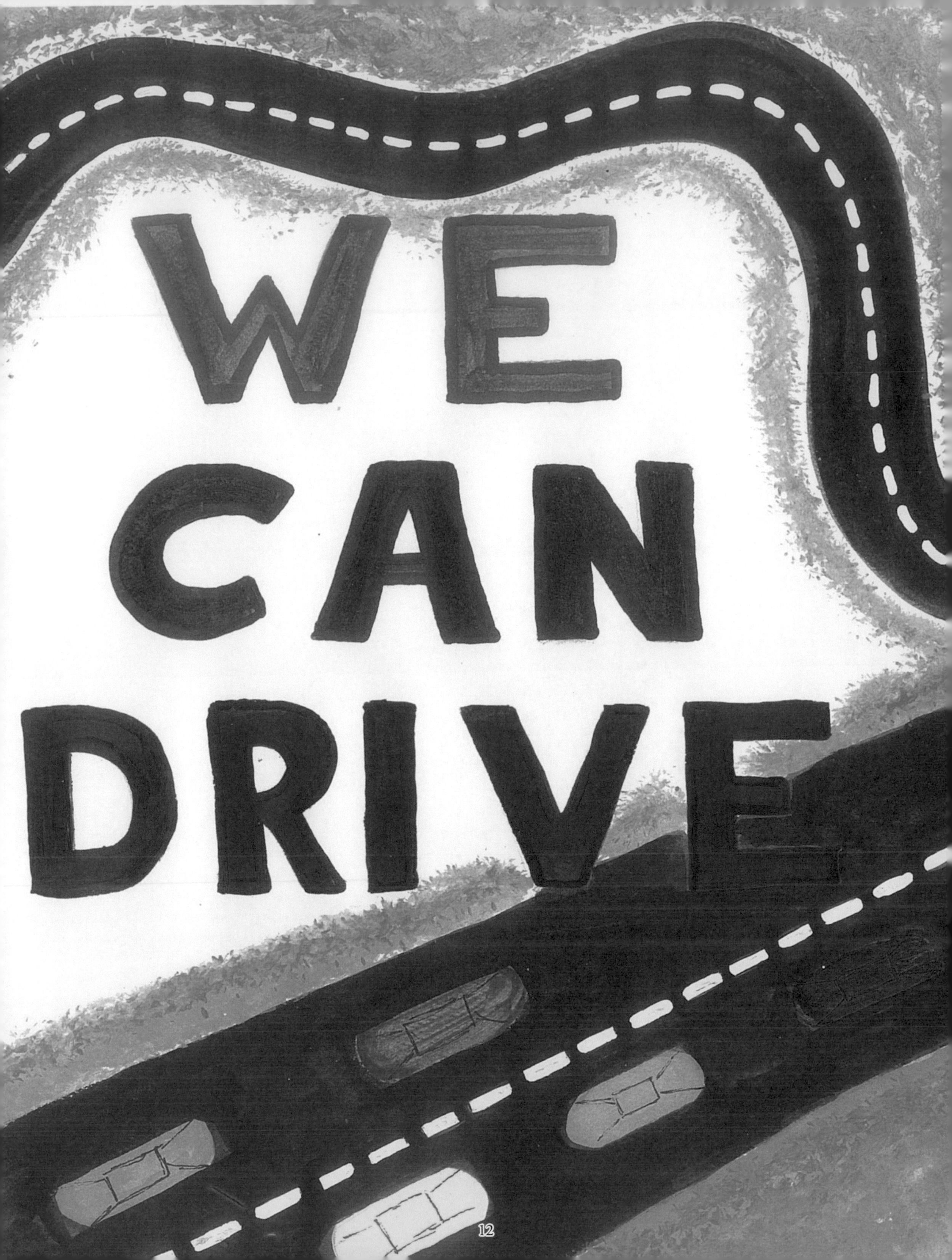
WE
CAN
DRIVE

"Grandpa, Grandpa... how come you can drive and not I? Oh why... Oh why...?"

"Little one, sit on my lap and take the wheel,
only grown-ups drive, so this is a big deal?"
"We will drive around and go real far.
That is the joy of driving this car."
"So, hop on in and let's get it in gear, this is the
best time of the year. It's not too hot and it's not
too cold and driving a car never gets old."

So off they go all around the town. Grandpa's girl is all smiles with not one single frown. They drove past the movie theater and even the bank. She is so grateful with Grandpa to thank. "Slow down, my little one, ease up on the gas, one must never drive too fast."

"Grandpa, Grandpa... this is so much fun.
But look we're driving with no sun."

In the blink of an eye, it has started to rain, now drive towards that road and head for the main. People are waving and yelling out loud; Grandpa's girl is driving and Grandpa's real proud. With umbrella's in hand they all walk really fast. The rain is so hard it's no longer a blast.

"Grandpa, Grandpa... what shall I do?" "Just don't start to cry and no boohoo's." The rain has let up, but it started to snow. Which way will they head, which way should they go?

The snow came down harder and the car went into a skid. This isn't something that's meant for a kid.

"I think it's time for me to take over and drive, this has become a very scary ride."

"Grandpa, Grandpa... please still let me drive, you are so nervous, your breaking out in hives!"

She closes her eyes and
continued to go,
up ahead is a
Rainbow...

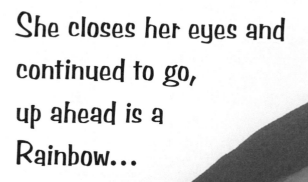

She drives to the
end with all that
she got and over the
other side, straight into
the pot...

The car starts to sink into a tub of gold. So much money they could not hold.

"Grandpa, Grandpa… we are so rich. Can we keep the money and hide it in a ditch?"

"Little one, little one… this isn't ours to keep. It must stay in this pot or our car will sink in deep."

"Now the drive is over and we must give this car a rest.

And always remember, my little one, that Grandpa will always love you the best!"

As Legends say,

"At the end of the rainbow there's a Pot of Gold".

It's not for us to take... it's for the very old.

How old do you have to be they shouted?

That's the mystery little Emma, because we really don't know.

— Joseph C. Pepe (Great Grandpa Papa Joe)

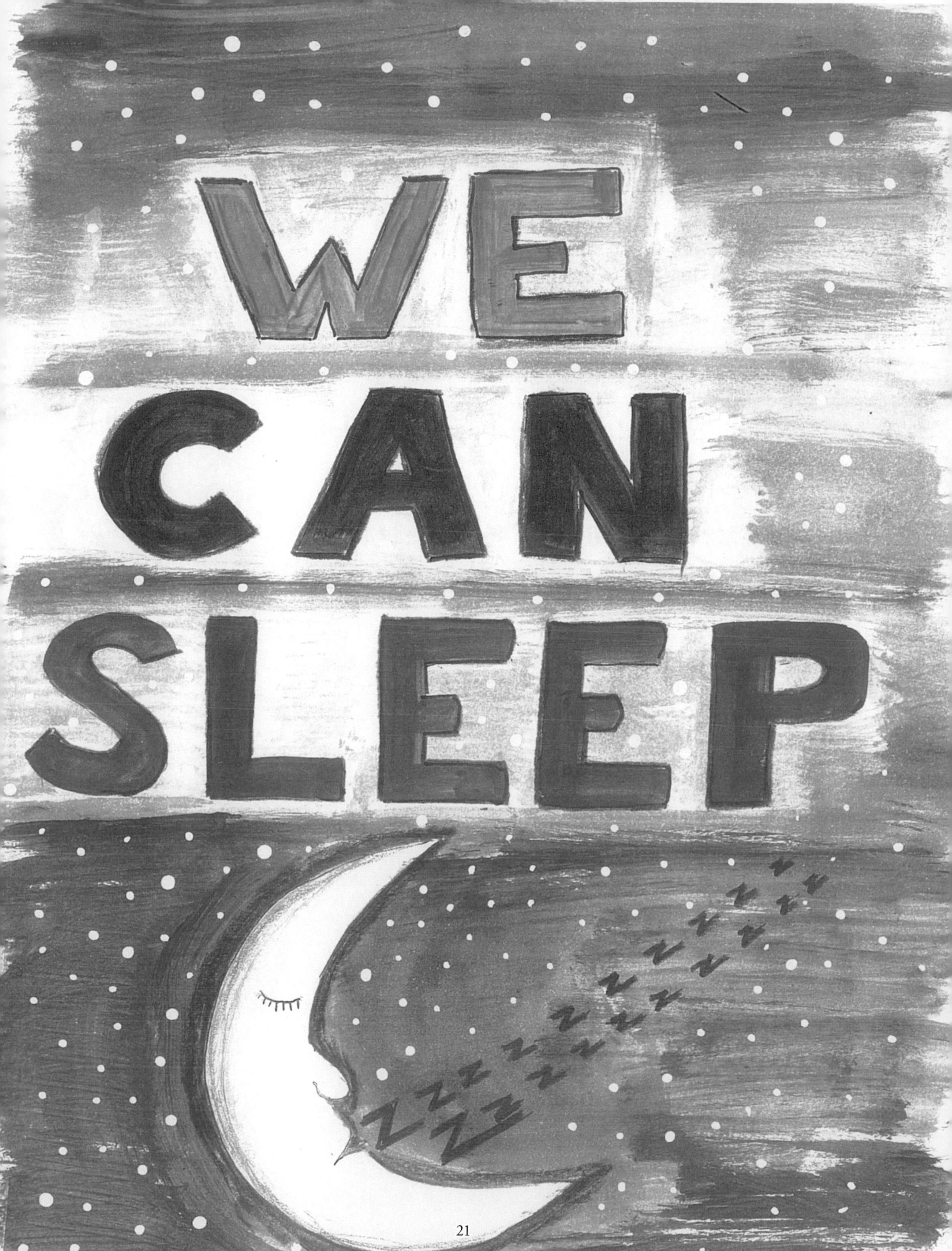
WE
CAN
SLEEP

"Grandpa, Grandpa... why can't we stay awake and not go to sleep?" "Because your body needs rest so you can take a leap."

"Let's shut your eyes tight and drift away, let Grandpa show you another way."

Together they fall asleep, their bodies relax and they're off into a deep sleep.

First, they enter the cave of gloom. Grandpa's girl holds Grandpa's hand and senses doom.

"Don't be afraid, my little one, there's nothing to fear. Grandpa is close and always near. Look at the pebbles, don't let go of my hand.

Up ahead is the Sandman....

He enters your room when you're starting to sleep. In fact, you are counting sheep from 'Little Bo Peep'. He sprinkles soft sand that falls in your eyes, it tickles the lids and doesn't make you cry.

When he's done with his work, he vanishes to dust. Every night he visits you.

Every night is a must!"

We lightly snore and continue to dream, let's go on the next mission and follow the beam.

Sheep in the pasture, cows that jump over the moon, an owl in the tree that's Hooting at me.

They follow us in the meadow and there's more than we can count. The numbers so large, a huge amount.

Up ahead there's a little girl named Emma behind the tree. What is she looking at? Does she see me?

"Grandpa, Grandpa... why does she hide? We won't hurt her. I'd like to bring her on our ride."

Up the valleys down the peaks, they travel along for what feels like weeks.

"Grandpa, Oh Grandpa... Can we move along? Or maybe you can sing me one more song."

HOOT HOOT

Grandpa started to sing his favorite tune. The one from the movie that lasso's the moon.

The song is from "It's a Wonderful Life" and it's "Buffalo Girl", the music makes her want to twirl.

Light on her feet and dance to the beat, Grandpa's voice is really neat.

"Dance with me Grandpa and spin me around, then lift me up off the ground."

Together in sleep they move so swiftly, in this dream they are so nifty.

She starts to stir, could she be beginning to wake? She turns to her other side and now they're by a lake.

This lake never ends, it goes on forever. Only in a dream, can it get any better. "Step off the land and walk out on the water, be brave, little one, like your mother who is my daughter."

Tiptoeing on the water, "please don't let us sink, if we start to go under, we'll have no time to think."

"Silly Grandpa's girl, I won't let this be, it will always be you and me. "

"BUFFALO GIRL"

Opening her eyes, she is starting to wake, was it a dream, she doesn't know what to make.

Looking over at Grandpa, who has also awoke.

Sleeping isn't just for us old folks.

She leans over to take a peek; he sees her smile from cheek to cheek.

"I told you don't worry and now we are done."

She said, "sleeping and dreaming are so much fun."

He smiles back to think where they begun. She tells "Grandpa, you will always be my number one."

"Grandpa, Grandpa... why do bees and birds fly and not I?
Oh Why... Oh Why?"
"Birds and bees can fly, little one.

Close your eyes and say, "Oh my"
See us soar so way up high, just like the birds and bees up
in the sky."

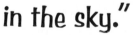

"Oh my…. Oh my….! Grandpa, Grandpa….!
Yes, I can see, we are so high above the trees."
"Hold my hand, little one, so you stay close.
I have somewhere you'll love the most."
They fly through the air with the greatest of ease, with an
excited grandpa's girl so easy to please.

Arms straight out like the wings of an eagle. Grandpa's
change in his pocket starts to jingle. First through the parks
and onto the city, Grandpa's girl finds it witty.

"Grandpa, Grandpa… your coins will fall, other children will
find them and have a ball."

Soon they land a top the largest skyscraper, the tallest Grandpa has seen in the paper.
"Open your eyes and what do you see?"
"Grandpa, Grandpa…. I see it all. Some are big and some are small.

Are those ants I see below?"
Grandpa chuckles and tells her "no." "Those are people down below."
"I see, I see…! This is so much fun! Grandpa, you'll always be my number one!"

"Now, now little one, you are still small. Let's just wait until you're tall. Stretch out your arms and here we go. There's so much more for you to know. So close your eyes and grab my hand, as we fly above this beautiful land." On through the woods and way past the prairies, soon it is night and there will be fairies.

"Grandpa, Oh Grandpa… The fairies are so pretty. They are smiling at me and making me giddy.

Can we take one home with us? I promise not to fuss. I'll hide her so she can't be seen, and I'll let her out when I dream."

"Silly little one, with such imagination. Fairies need to be free to glide through the nations. America, Africa and even Japan, fairies wave such colorful fans."

"Off we go, it's getting late, we can always plan another date. Close your eyes and we'll fly back home. Pass the stars we'll try not to roam."

Minutes later, we're back in her bedroom. Tiptoeing in the dark through the light of the moon.

"Shush…shush… let's not make noise, be careful not to trip over your toys."

"Hee-hee, tsk, tsk, we saw so much. Tomorrow can we fly to Europe to see the Dutch?"

"We have a lot of time I'll always be here, now let me tuck you in my dear."

"Tomorrow will be here, so get some rest. Grandpa will always love you the best."

Printed in the United States
By Bookmasters